This book belongs to

_____

_____

Aged _____

STORIES FOR THE YOUNG READER

Peter Meets a Dragon

AND OTHER STORIES

Peter Meets a Dragon

AND OTHER STORIES

p

This is a Parragon Book
This edition published in 2001

Parragon
Queen Street House
4 Queen Street
Bath BA1 1HE, UK

Copyright © Parragon 2000

ISBN 0-75253-410-6

Designed by Mik Martin

Printed in Italy

These stories have been previously
published by Parragon in the
Bumper Bedtime Series 1999

CONTENTS

Peter
Meets a
Dragon

ONCE UPON A TIME there was a young boy named Peter. He lived in an ordinary house with an ordinary Mum and Dad, an ordinary sister and an ordinary pet cat, called Jasper. In fact, everything in Peter's life was so ordinary that he sometimes wished that something extraordinary would happen. "Why doesn't a giant come and squash the house flat with his foot?" he wondered, and "If only a pirate would take my sister hostage!" But each day, Peter would wake up in the morning and everything was just the same as it had been the day before.

One morning Peter woke up to find a very strange smell in the house. Looking out of his bedroom window, he saw that the front lawn was scorched and blackened. There was smoke drifting off the grass and, further away, he could see some bushes ablaze.

Peter rushed downstairs and out of the front door. He ran out of the garden and down the lane following the trail of smoke and burning grass. He grew more and more puzzled, however, as there was no sign of anything that could have caused such a blaze.

Peter was about to run home and tell his Mum and Dad, when he heard a panting noise coming from the undergrowth. Parting the bushes gently with his hands he found a young creature. It had green, scaly skin, a pair of wings and a long snout full of sharp teeth. Every now and again a little tongue of flame came from its nostrils, setting the grass around it on fire. "A baby dragon!" Peter said to himself, in great surprise. Big tears were rolling out of the dragon's yellow eyes and down its scaly cheeks as it flapped its wings desperately and tried to take off.

When the dragon saw Peter it stopped flapping its wings.

"Oh, woe is me!" it sobbed. "Where am I?"

"Where do you want to be?"

asked Peter, kneeling down on the scorched ground.

"I want to be in Dragonland with my friends," replied the dragon. "We were all flying together, but I just couldn't keep up with them. I got tired and needed a rest. I called to the others but they didn't hear me. Then I just had to stop and get my breath back. Now I don't know where I am, or if I'll ever see my

friends again!" And with that the baby dragon started to cry once more.

"I'm sure I can help. I'll get you home," said Peter, though he had no idea how.

"You?" hissed a voice nearby. "How could you possibly help? You're just a boy!" Peter looked round, and to his astonishment found Jasper sitting behind him. "I suppose you're going to wave a magic wand, are you?" continued Jasper. "You need to call in an expert." Then he turned his back on Peter and the baby dragon and started washing his paws.

Peter was astounded. He'd never

heard Jasper talking before. He had thought he was just an ordinary pet cat. "W… w… what do you mean?" he stammered.

"Well," said Jasper, glancing over his shoulder at Peter, "I reckon that horse over there could help. Follow me."

So Peter and the baby dragon — whose name was Flame — followed Jasper over to where the horse stood at the edge of a field. Jasper leaped up on to the gate and called to the horse. Then he whispered in the horse's ear. The horse thought for a moment, then whispered back in Jasper's ear.

"He says he's got a friend on the

other side of the wood who'll help," said Jasper.

"But how?" said Peter, looking perplexed.

"Be patient! Follow me!" said Jasper as he stalked off through the grass. "And tell your friend to stop setting fire to everything!" he added. Peter saw, to his horror, that Flame was indeed blazing a trail through the field.

"I can't help it," cried Flame, about to burst into tears again. "Every time I get out of breath I start to pant, and then I start breathing fire."

"Let me carry you," said Peter. He picked Flame up in his arms and ran after Jasper. The baby dragon felt very strange. His body was all cold and clammy, but his mouth was still breathing hot smoke, which made Peter's eyes water.

He ran through the wood, just keeping Jasper's upright tail in sight. On the other side of the wood was another field, and in the field was a horse. But this was no ordinary horse. Peter stopped dead in his tracks and stared. The horse was pure milky white, and from its head grew a single, long horn. "A unicorn!" breathed Peter.

Jasper was already talking to the unicorn. He beckoned with his paw to Peter. "He'll take your friend home and you can go, too, Peter, but don't be late for tea, or you know what your mother will say." And with that, Jasper was off.

"Climb aboard," said the unicorn gently.

Peter and the little dragon scrambled up on to the unicorn's back. "What an adventure," thought Peter. Up, up, and away they soared through the clouds.

Flame held tightly on to Peter's hand with his clammy paw. At last Peter could see a mountain ahead through the clouds. Now they were descending through the clouds again, and soon the unicorn landed right at the top of the mountain.

"I'm home!" squeaked Flame joyously
as they landed. Sure enough, several
dragons were running over to greet
him. They looked quite friendly, but
some of them were rather large
and one was breathing a great deal
of fire.

"Time for me to go," said Peter a
little nervously, as Flame jumped off
the unicorn's back and flew to the
ground. The unicorn took off again
and soon they were back in the field
once more.

As he slid off the unicorn's
back, Peter turned to thank him, but
when he looked he saw that it was
just an ordinary horse with no trace
of a horn at all. Peter walked back

home across the field, but there was no sign of burnt grass. He reached his own front lawn, which was also in perfect condition. Peter felt more and more perplexed. "I hope Jasper can explain," he thought, as the cat ran past him and into the house.

"Jasper, I took the baby dragon home. What's happened to the burnt grass?" he blurted out. But Jasper said not a word. He ignored Peter and curled up in his basket.

When Peter wasn't looking, however, Jasper gave him a glance that seemed to say, "Well, was that a big enough adventure for you?"

The Good Goblin

Written by Candy Wallace

DEEP IN THE HEART of a great forest, a long way away and a long time ago, lived a gang of goblins. Most of them were just like goblins everywhere — horrible.

Small goblins attended school to learn how to be nasty. Soon they were taking exams in Telling Lies, Cheating, General Nastiness 1 and 2, Sneering and Loathing. The goblins who were better at doing things with their hands took Pinching, Punching and Stealing Things. If a goblin passed all his exams he got a Certificate in Nastiness and became a fully qualified goblin.

One of them, however, didn't quite fit in. His name was Pookie and he never managed to pass a single exam. When Question 1 said, "Describe, in not more than one hundred words, how you would steal a little girl's birthday cake," he wrote, "Well, actually I wouldn't do that because it's not really an awfully nice thing to do."

Question 4 said, "How would you make someone feel really miserable? Would you a. laugh at their skinny legs, b. trip them up, or c. give them a cuddle?" Pookie wrote, "Give them a cuddle," and got nought out of twenty.

The goblins used to go out on

stealing expeditions. You know the
sort of thing, making off with one
sock so someone spends the next
week trying to find it and ends up

with not one matching pair. Or sneaking into a little boy's bedroom and taking his favourite toy.

All the other goblins had given up on Pookie. They left him behind on these outings because as fast as they were stealing things, Pookie was taking them back. Once they returned and found he'd washed all their nicely grimy clothes and put them out to dry in the sunshine. He was absolutely impossible.

They tried taking him to the goblin doctor. "Can you give Pookie some medicine to make him nastier?" they asked.

"Well, young goblin," said the doctor to Pookie gravely, "I'm afraid this medicine is going to taste nice, but unless a medicine tastes nice, it won't do you any good at all. You'll have to be brave and take it every day."

Pookie said the doctor was very kind and promised to follow his instructions

A week later the goblins went to visit Pookie to see if he had become any nastier.

"We're off to rip holes in shopping bags so all the food falls out!" they said to him, temptingly. "You'll enjoy that won't you, Pookie?"

"It's very good of you to invite me," replied Pookie, "but I promised a blackbird I'd help her make her nest today. I'm most frightfully sorry." And off he went, whistling a happy tune.

Nothing seemed to work. It was time to try something drastic.

"We'll go and ask the wizard to sort him out!" they cried.

"He's the only one who can make Pookie nasty!"

Sure enough, in a cave near the forest lived an old wizard called Woozle. Woozle had a terrible temper and usually threw things at the goblins when they came near. But many's the time the goblins had seen him chanting and mixing strange potions. They saw him turn a snail into a teapot and a.rabbit into a toothbrush. Changing a nice goblin into a nasty goblin should be a piece of cake for a clever wizard like him.

This was certainly a challenge for a wizard of genius and creative brilliance such as himself.

What the goblins didn't know was that Woozle wasn't very good at casting spells and was always getting into trouble. There was that embarrassing episode when he'd turned his Uncle Tertius into a pig, not to mention the unfortunate incident when he tried to magic his donkey into a horse. The next thing he knew there was a one-hundred-

and-sixty-pound centipede tied up outside his cave.

He was wrestling with a spell to make acorns into cupcakes when the goblins approached him, nervously, one morning. Luckily for the goblins the wizard was in a good mood. He;d managed to turn his budgie into a chocolate chip cookie, so he felt he was on the right track.

"We need your help," they said, and explained about Pookie. "He's a very bad influence on the younger goblins," they told him. "There must be something you can do." The wizard looked thoughtful.

"All right, I'll do it," said Woozle.

"I'll come over tomorrow with one of my magic potions. I'm sure it will be the simplest of matters to transform this poor, deluded young goblin into a fine, unpleasant young goblin. Leave it to me!"

The next day, all the goblins gathered together in a clearing to wait for the wizard's arrival. Pookie strolled along too, curious as to why everyone was so excited. Then he noticed they were all sniggering and pointing at him and he began to feel rather uncomfortable.

At last, the wizard arrived on foot. He was going to come on his centipede, but had changed his mind. It was a very obliging

centipede and much better
tempered than the donkey had
been, but Woozle felt rather seasick
whenever he tried to ride on him.
It must have been all those legs.

So, when he arrived, the wizard
was rather tired. He sat down on a
rock puffing and blowing and
coughing.

"I've ... brought ... the ...
potion," he wheezed and wiped his
brow. Reaching into his pocket he
took out a little bottle with bright
yellow liquid in it. "Where is the
goblin in question?"

Instantly, Pookie knew it was
him. He found himself pushed
forwards by the other goblins.

The wizard drew a chalk circle around Pookie and asked all the other goblins to stand around him and hold hands. Then he sprinkled the yellow mixture around the chalk circle.

Woozle took out a pair of wire spectacles and balanced them on his nose. Then he pulled out a tattered piece of paper covered

in scribbles.

"Er, yes now, here it is, er, ah yes, here is nice where should be nasty, change this situation fasty!" The wizard took his specs off and coughed nervously. "Poetry was never my strong point," he apologised.

Nevertheless, he felt pleased. He looked at Pookie hopefully for signs of a sneer. But Pookie wasn't looking at him. Pookie was looking at all the other goblins. They were dancing towards the wizard, hand-in-hand.

"Thanks most awfully for coming to see us!" said one. "Have a nice cup of tea before you go," cried another.

"Do forgive us," said the Chief Goblin. "I'm afraid we can't stay, we simply must dash and help some old ladies cross the road. Good morning to you!"

The goblins skipped off happily down the path, pausing only to pick daisies and wave at passing butterflies.

Pookie and the wizard were left, staring in astonishment. They looked at each other and gulped.

"That was a very good spell, Mr Wizard," said Pookie at last. "You must be the cleverest wizard in the whole world."

Woozle put his spectacles

away. He thought it was a good
spell to finish his wizard career. It
was time to take up gardening.

Wobbly Witch

Written by Candy Wallace

WOBBLY WITCH had a problem. She was wobbly. She wasn't wobbly when she walked down to the bottom of the garden to pick toadstools. And she wasn't wobbly when she stood over her cauldron mixing the latest recipes from *What Spell?* magazine, or when she sat on her little stool by the fire and toasted rats' tails for tea. But, when she tried to fly anywhere on her broomstick — she wobbled. She wobbled and swayed and clutched and shrieked and fell to the ground in a horrible heap!

Poor Wobbly had never learned to fly a broomstick. Some witches took to it like a duck to water and never needed a single lesson. Others went to the *Sky's The Limit School of Broomstick Flying*. But Wobbly just couldn't be bothered to learn when she was young and now she was too proud to admit that she couldn't fly. She told all her friends that she'd lost her broomstick.

So Wobbly had to go everywhere on the bus. It was very embarrassing and most inconvenient. How would you feel if you had to sit on a bus in your pointy black hat with horrid schoolboys making rude remarks about your funny nose? She even had to go to the W.I. (the Witches' Institute) on the bus. All the others flew in on smart broomsticks. Wobbly felt quite left out as they discussed the special features of their latest models.

"Mine does 0-60 in ten seconds," said Edna.

Wobbly might never have learned to fly, if it hadn't been for the birthday present and her cat, Boris.

On Wobbly's birthday the postman brought lots of lovely birthday cards, a couple of small parcels and one big one that was very long and very thin. One parcel had a smart new witch's hat in it, from Wobbly's friend Vera.

The other one was a silver balloon on a string. It had "Happy Birthday!" on it and floated up into the air when she opened the parcel. Wobbly was very pleased.

"Now what can this long one be, Boris?" said Wobbly to her cat, who, like all cats was very curious. Boris snuggled up to Wobbly and purred. He'd had a large kipper for breakfast and was in a very good mood.

Wobbly opened the long thin parcel and her heart sank to her big black boots. It was a spanking new, super deluxe broomstick with built-in stereo and cat seat! "To Wobbly," said the card, "with love from all your friends at the Witches' Institute."

Wobbly hurriedly wrapped it up again and stuffed the broomstick under the bed. "Stupid present," she muttered. "I hate birthdays." And she didn't cheer up until Boris rolled on his back and made her chuckle.

That night the W.I. were meeting. Wobbly went on the bus, as usual.

"I'll tell them I forgot my broomstick," she said to herself. When she arrived, there was a big surprise — her friends had laid on a lovely birthday party for her.

"Happy Birthday, Wobbly!" they shouted as she came in the door.

"Where's your lovely new broom-stick?"

Wobbly soon forgot to feel miserable. There was a huge birthday cake decorated with little bats made out of icing. There were extra wobbly jellies in her honour and lots of delicious sandwiches. It all went well, until somebody mentioned playing games.

They played Hide and Shriek, Pass the Toad and Pin the Tail on the Rat. But the next game was Broomstick Races. Soon, all the witches but Wobbly were whizzing up and down on their broomsticks, cackling and having fun. Wobbly looked on and sulked.

"Right, that's it!" she said. "I'm going home. I hate parties!" And she sneaked out. When she arrived home, she expected Boris to meet her at the door. But there was no sign of him.

"Great lazy lump," thought Wobbly, crossly. "He's still sleeping off that kipper I gave him!" But when she looked on his favourite chair, he wasn't there. "Boris, Boris,

where are you?" she called. But there was no answering miaow.

Feeling worried, Wobbly went outside and called his name again. It was a dark night with a bright, shiny moon and she strained her eyes to see. Then something caught her eye. Right at the top of a tree, she saw a flash of light. It was her birthday balloon, caught on a branch. Suddenly, the branch shook.

"Miaeeeeeew!" It was Boris! He had chased the balloon to the top of the tallest tree in the garden and now he was stuck!

"Oh, you silly cat!" shrieked Wobbly. "How am I going to get you down from there!"

"Miaeeeeeew!" wailed poor Boris.

Wobbly rushed to fetch an old ladder. But when she put it against the tree it didn't even reach half way up. Poor Boris seemed to be clinging on by a claw. His miaows grew fainter...

Wobbly stamped her foot and turned and rushed into her cottage. She dashed up the stairs and into the bedroom.

On her hands and knees, she grabbed the parcel under the bed and hurried downstairs with it, tearing off the paper as she went.

"Don't worry, Boris!" she cried. "I'll rescue you!" Leaping astride the gleaming new broomstick, she closed her eyes and took a deep breath…

Up she went, up into the sky without a single wobble! As she climbed higher and higher, her old hat blew off and was carried away by the wind. The broomstick swept round in a curve and came to a stop, hovering over the branch where poor Boris was clinging on for dear life.

Wobbly grabbed him and put him on the broomstick behind her. Then she untangled the balloon, tied it to the broomstick and swept down to a smooth landing outside her front door. Boris walked off the broomstick as if nothing had happened.

Wobbly leapt off and skipped and hopped with glee.

"Did you see that, Boris!" she cackled. "I can fly, I can fly! Come on!" She ran into the cottage and grabbed her new hat. "We have a party to go to!"

They jumped back on and took off.

"I've fetched my new broomstick!" cried Wobbly as she arrived at the party. They were still racing broomsticks and hadn't even noticed she was gone! Wobbly and Boris joined in and won two races! As they flew home after the party,

Wobbly looked down at the bus below and chuckled.

"I couldn't fly because I was afraid," she said to Boris, who sat purring behind her. "But tonight

I was so worried you would fall and hurt yourself — I forgot to be afraid!"

From that day on, Wobbly flew everywhere on her smart new broomstick. She's still called Wobbly, but she doesn't wobble any more!

A Dog
Named
Brian

Written by Candy Wallace

WIMPLE THE WITCH was having trouble with her cat. Now, as you know, all witches need a cat. No cat, no spells. They just won't work without the magic spark from a cat's eyes. So when Wimple had trouble with her cat — it was big trouble.

"You're a great big useless heap of fur," she shrieked at Montgomery, who was lying on his back with his paws in the air, snoring. "Can't you think of anything better to do than sleep all day?"

Wimple drew back her large foot and booted him across the room — no mean feat since Montgomery weighed nearly as much as a sack of coal. Montgomery rotated in mid-air twice and came to rest on his paws with a faint look of surprise.

His feelings were more hurt than anything. True, he had slowed down a trifle lately, but frankly, he was getting on a bit now. He'd used up eight-and-a-half lives and all he wanted was a bit of peace.

Wimple put her hands on her hips and glowered at Montgomery, who had keeled over on the spot and fallen into an instant slumber.

"Right!" she screamed. "That's it!" It was time to get another cat. One she could rely on. In two shakes of a rat's tail she was astride her broomstick and on her way to the *Paws for Thought* cat agency.

"I want a sleek, hardworking black cat with a flash of genius. Experience in turning princes into frogs and vice versa would be preferred," she said, to the bored-looking witch behind the counter.

"No," the assistant said.

"What do you mean — no?" said Wimple.

"No cats left on our books. We've had a run on them this week."

Wimple turned purple.

"All we've got left is a dog called Brian." While Wimple stood there, speechless, the assistant went into a back room and came back with a huge bloodhound who looked rather depressed. He knew just what would happen. They always took one look at him and shrieked with laughter.

He'd spent three years learning to be a Witch's Personal Assistant and now nobody would hire him.

"I'll take him!" said Wimple suddenly. She was a desperate witch. "I just wish he wasn't quite so big."

The first problem was that there was no way Brian was going to ride on the broomstick. When he got on it it just wouldn't budge. So poor Wimple had to walk all the way home, carrying her broomstick with Brian lolloping along behind.

Back home, she decided to try him out straight away on a spell. She had an excellent recipe brewing in the cauldron, designed to turn bacon sandwiches into roast beef with roast potatoes,

Yorkshire pudding and Brussel sprouts, her favourite meal.

"Right — er — Brian, all you have to do is sit there and stare at the cauldron until it starts to bubble." Brian looked quietly confident. He'd passed Cauldron Staring with grade A.

"I'll go and find that good-for-nothing cat and tell him he's fired!"

Brian sat and stared dutifully at the cauldron. It was a very big cauldron and even Brian couldn't see inside it. So he didn't know whether it was bubbling or not. He thought he'd better check and put his paws up on the top of the cauldron to look in. The big pot swayed and tilted and crash! It toppled over. All the bubbling liquid flowed onto the floor — and over Montgomery who was busy escaping from Wimple.

Montgomery felt very strange for a minute and then turned into a Brussel sprout. Wimple, following behind, stopped dead in her tracks.

"You stupid dog! Quick, we'll have to mix another spell." She thumbed through her recipe book until she found Brussel Sprout — Into Cat, page 62. "We need some toadstools. Go and get some this minute!" Poor Brian was feeling very embarrassed and loped off into the garden, determined he would prove himself this time. He came back carrying a basket full of toadstools.

Strangely enough, Wimple didn't seem pleased. She was staring out of the window with eyes like saucers, clenching her fists.

"You've — just — trampled — all — over — my — magic — herbs," she said, very slowly. "The

ones that have taken me a year to grow…"

Brian thought that now would be a good time to disappear for a while.

When Wimple had calmed down, she mixed the spell, muttering to herself about stupid dogs and cats, and managed to restore Montgom-ery to his previous furry self, none the worse for wear. But then she dropped her recipe book into the cauldron and it disintegrated in a puff of smoke.

That was the last straw. Wimple was literally hopping mad. She jumped up and down and stamped her feet, hopping all over the room.

Then bump! Her head hit the shelf where she kept all her secret jars and bottles.

A big dusty jar marked Frog Mixture teetered on the brink, then fell over, the thick green liquid pouring down onto Wimple's head.

When Brian and Montgomery crept in a little later, Wimple didn't seem to be there. There was just this small, rather bewildered frog sitting on the floor.

Brian looked up at the shelf where all the bottles were higgledy piggledy and saw the upturned jar. He looked at Montgomery and Montgomery looked at him. Then they both looked at the frog.

They ran over to where Wimple's recipe book was kept, but there was no sign of it anywhere! Brian and Montgomery would just have to try and remember the right spell between them. Montgomery rushed out into the garden and nibbled off some squashed herbs. Brian took down the jar marked Pickled Slugs and another that said

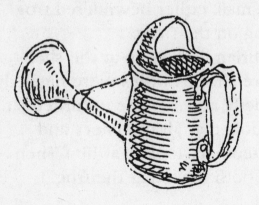

All Purpose Slime — Top Quality.
They mixed all the ingredients
together in a spare pot and stirred
it with their paws. The frog looked
on and blinked silently. Together,
the cat and dog sat and stared hard
at the pot. Slowly, it began to
bubble. With that, the frog made a
sudden leap and landed in the pot
with a plop.

And out came — Wimple! She
was a little slimy, to be sure, but it
was definitely her. When she'd dried
herself off and had a couple of
chocolate biscuits, she felt much
better. Wimple sat on her wooden
stool and patted Montgomery and
Brian on the head.

"I was wrong about you two," she said finally. "A witch couldn't have two better assistants." She shuddered as she remembered sitting on the floor with green skin and big feet. She would never turn anyone into a frog again. After she'd thrown away all the frog mixture she could find, she found a big juicy bone for Brian and a tasty kipper for Montgomery. "What a team!" she cackled and tucked in to her roast beef and Yorkshire pudding.

The Worst Witches

Written by Ian Tabor

THE WITCHES Mog, Marge and Mable were useless. If they tried to turn someone into a frog, he turned into a prince and if they tried to turn someone into a prince he turned into a frog. At Witch School they had only been given their diplomas so that they wouldn't come back the following year.

Now they sat round a boiling cauldron in a forest clearing looking extremely down in the mouth.

"I do wish that we could do something right for once," wailed Mog.

"The trouble is," said Marge,

"almost everyone has heard how useless we are. Nobody in their right mind would employ us."

"Hey, listen to this," said Mable letting out a cackle. "DRAGON HOLDS KING TO RANSOM. A mad fire-breathing dragon is rampaging through the land burning all trees before him. The dragon, known simply as Inferno, has said that he will only stop when the king gives him his daughter's hand in marriage. The king has refused and has called on all the brave knights in the kingdom to slay the dragon."

"Ooh!" exclaimed Mog. "We haven't had a dragon in the area for ages. What fun!"

"Not if he's burning down all of our trees it isn't!" said Marge.

"Well if you ask me," said Mable, "this is our chance to show everyone that we're not just three useless old witches. We must stop the dragon, then we'll be heroines."

"But how?"

"Good question. Tell you what, why don't we have a think over a bowl of my nice soup." And giving the cauldron one final stir Mable ladled the thick, green soup into three bowls. "What exactly is in this?" asked Marge, peering cautiously into her bowl, which was boiling and bubbling.

"Oh a little bit of this and a

little bit of that," replied Mable
mysteriously. "It's actually a new
recipe that I've just made up."

The three witches sipped their
soup, trying to think of a way to
destroy the evil dragon.

"What's that?" said Mog,
looking up from her bowl of soup.

"What's what?" asked Marge.

"That sound. It's a flap, flap,
flapping sort of a noise," Mog said,
nervously.

"I can hear it as well," said
Mable. "But where's it coming from?"

The noise was getting louder
and louder. Suddenly Mog let out a
piercing scream and pointed to the
sky.

Marge and Mable followed her warty finger and there, above them, was the dragon.

"Run!" screamed Mog. "Run before we're fried!" In a mad panic they tried to run away from the monster but all they succeeded in doing was running into each other. Their bowls of soup went flying through the air and landed in the forest. Mog, Marge and Mable ended up in a jumbled heap on the ground.

The dragon swooped down letting out a scorching jet of fire. The witches screamed, but it was too late. Just as the flame was about to reach them and turn them into cinders the three witches fainted.

When Mog woke up she couldn't believe her eyes. The forest was just a smoldering lump of charcoal, all that is, except for three trees.

"Marge! Mable! Wake up!" she cried, poking the other two. "We didn't get burnt. We're alive."

The other two sat up, blinking in disbelief.

"And look," said Mog, pointing to the unharmed trees. "How do you think they survived?"

"It's a miracle!" exclaimed Mable.

"Close," said Marge. "It was your soup, Mable. Look. There's one of our soup bowls at the bottom of each tree. It might not be all that wonderful for eating," Marge said with a smile, "but your soup makes things fire-proof. You're a genius, Mable!"

"I am?" said Mable, looking at Marge in amazement.

"This is our chance to be heroines," said Marge. "If we can protect the trees, then the dragon's powers will be useless."

"Come on," said Mog. "We haven't a moment to lose. We must go and see the king."

The king was feeling very miserable when the witches arrived and willingly agreed to their plan. All of his knights had ended in a puddle of melted metal. The witches were his last chance.

Huge cauldrons were brought up from the royal kitchens and Mable, with the help of Mog and Marge, began making the special soup. Soon they had made over one hundred cauldrons full of soup. The king gave orders for one drop to be dripped on every tree in the kingdom and for each person to be given one mouthful.

The next time the dragon came he got quite a surprise. He huffed and he puffed but he couldn't get even one small tree to catch alight. In the end he gave up and went back to his lair cursing the witches. The king was overjoyed.

"Well done! Well done indeed!" he exclaimed. "Not only have you saved all the trees in the kingdom, but my daughter will not have to marry that evil dragon. You are now my official royal witches."

Mog, Marge and Mable grinned in delight. Perhaps they weren't so useless after all.

A Monster Hit

Written by Candy Wallace

IT WAS a Tuesday when Kevin discovered there was a monster living in the television. He had just settled down to watch his favourite cartoon programme with a ginormous glass of lemonade and a jumbo packet of crisps.

Reggie the cat had been sleeping peacefully on the rug, ears and whiskers twitching as he dreamed happily of a wrestling match with a giant mouse, where, as usual, the score was Reggie 1, Mouse 0. Everything normal then, in Kevin's house.

Kevin took a huge mouthful of crisps and a big gulp of lemonade and settled down to watch *The*

Adventures of Fancy Frog, a gripping tale of a gentleman frog who wore a spotted bow tie and carried a walking cane.

This week, he was doing battle with Nasty Newt the pond gangster. It had just got to the bit where Fancy Frog was about to rescue a rather pretty goldfish in distress when a big hairy hand reached out of the back of the television and grabbed Kevin's packet of crisps. The packet disappeared back into the television and Kevin couldn't hear what Fancy Frog was saying for the noise of crunching crisps.

Reggie opened one eye and his

whiskers twitched towards the television like an aerial. His very pleasant dream had been interrupted and he had the strangest feeling that there was another animal in the room. Which was irritating because he would have to get up and growl and curve his back in a menacing sort of way and chase whatever it was down the garden path.

Kevin was annoyed about the crisps — and about missing his programme. It was just his luck to be the only boy in the street with a monster in his television. Then just as he was about to drink his lemonade, the giant hairy hand shot out of the television and grabbed it!

Glug, glug, glug went the television.
Then it burped.

"Mum!" shouted Kevin, really
fed up now. "Mum, there's a
monster in the television and it's
eaten my crisps and drunk my
lemonade!"

"Yes, dear," called Mum from the other room. "Your dad will fix it for you in a minute."

Kevin sighed. Dad had been trying all day to build some shelves in the garage. Every time he put them up they fell down again. Last time Kevin had seen Dad he had a purple face and was jumping up and down on a pile of wooden planks. Not the best time to ask Dad to get rid of a monster in the television. There wasn't likely to be a chapter on it in his DIY book either.

He decided to call his friend Eric.

"Hello, Eric, it's Kevin here. Yes,

I know Fancy Frog's on the telly at the moment, sorry. But I've got a monster in my television. Can you come round and give me a hand?"

When Kevin got back to the living room, Reggie was sitting on the top of the television with his head right down and his nose to the screen, mesmerised.

Fancy Frog had disappeared from the screen and instead there was a huge, horrible, hairy monster face, grinning and chuckling and poking its tongue out at Reggie. Reggie's fur was standing on end and he kept swiping at the face with his paw, but the monster was safely inside the screen.

Then Grandma came in.

"Is the weather on yet, dear?" she asked Kevin.

"No, sorry, Grandma," he answered. "I'm afraid we've got a monster in our television."

"But I always watch the weather!" said Grandma. "Can't you just change the channel?"

They tried, but the hairy monster was on every channel! Grandma decided she'd go next door and watch the weather on their television instead.

"Whatever is the world coming to?" she muttered.

The big hairy hand emerged.from the television again

and grabbed Reggie's tail. Before Kevin could stop him, the monster was swinging poor Reggie around before hurling him onto the sofa, where he landed in a crumpled heap.

The face on the TV screen croaked with glee. Reggie wasn't amused. He picked himself up, put his tail in the air, and with a disdainful sniff over his shoulder, stalked out of the room.

Just then, Eric arrived.

"Have you tried unplugging him?" he suggested helpfully. Kevin hadn't, so they tried. But the big hairy hand just shot out and plugged it in again. It was a real nuisance.

The neighbours came over
with Grandma to have a look at the
monster. Mr and Mrs Johnson had
several suggestions, from making a
citizen's arrest to calling the fire
brigade. But Kevin's mum thought
they might spray water all over her
nice new living room carpet.

The word soon spread that
there was a monster in the
television at number 28. Before long
there was a queue outside and
Kevin and Eric were organising
refreshments and doing a roaring
trade in cups of tea and Mum's
homemade scones. Dad didn't know
what was going on. He was still
trying to put up shelves in the

garage, but Mum helped Kevin put up a barrier with string around the television. This was after the monster grabbed Mrs Taylor's new hat and ate it in front of her on the screen, giggling as he did so. He even let out a big burp when he'd finished! Mrs Taylor was not impressed.

Two hours later a large van drew up outside and several people got out carrying cameras and microphones.

"Hello!" they shouted, as they marched through the front door, past the waiting neighbours and visitors.

"We're from TVB News. We've come to interview Kevin about the TV monster!"

"How long has this monster been in your television asked the lady reporter in a concerned voice. "Will this change your life? How do you feel?"

"Well, he's been here since Fancy Frog started about a quarter past five," replied Kevin.

"We feel really fed up because that's our favourite programme and it will change our life because

we'll have to go next door to
watch it."

The lady reporter nodded in a
caring sort of way.

"Thank you, Kevin. This is Anna
Badger-Jones at 28 Acacia Avenue,
reporting for TVB."

The next morning, Kevin was
invited onto breakfast television to
talk about his monster. The TV
company came and picked up
Kevin and his television with the
monster inside. In the studio they
plugged the monster in and asked
him questions about the world
situation. All he did was cackle and
croak and try and grab the cameras
with his big hairy hand, but he was

a big hit with the viewers. TVB
offered Kevin a brand new
television in return for leaving his
old television with them. They
wanted to give the monster his
own regular spot on the breakfast
show.

So after that Kevin and Eric
were able to watch Fancy Frog
every week and enjoy their crisps
and lemonade in peace. Now and
then, they would turn on the TV

before school and catch *The Mega Monster Show* where the monster had guests like pop stars and government ministers. Even Reggie would sit on the rug and watch, with an occasional twitch of his whiskers.

It was nice to see the monster now and again, but even nicer to be able to turn him off!

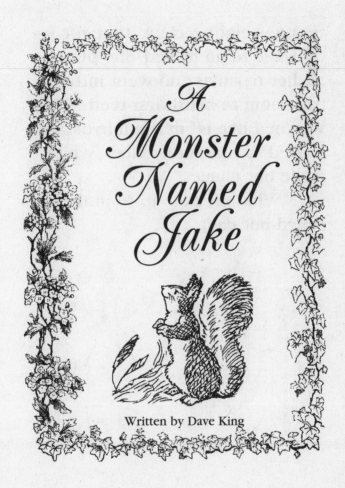

A Monster Named Jake

Written by Dave King

IT WAS eight o'clock, time for Katie to go to bed. She put on her pyjamas and went into the bathroom to brush her teeth. She watched herself in the mirror and started to pull funny faces, which made her giggle.

"What are you up to in there?" called her dad.

"Oh, nothing. Just brushing my teeth," Katie answered.

"Well, hurry up if you want a story," said Dad.

Katie wiped all the froth off her face and ran into her bedroom.

"About time," laughed Dad. "Which story shall we read tonight?"

"Mongo the Monster, please," said Katie.

"Oh, not again. Can't we have a different one?" moaned Dad.

"But it's my favourite," pleaded Katie.

Katie loved monsters. She had lots of monster books and toys and a huge poster of funny looking monsters on her wall. Katie thought the biggest one looked like Mongo in her story book.

Katie snuggled down and listened to her dad until he finished the story. As she lay there looking at her poster, wishing it was real and she could join the fun, she felt a little drowsy. She closed her eyes, and suddenly, she was standing by one of the trees in the poster and could hear the monsters talking.

"Has everybody arrived yet?" she heard Mongo ask, as he stomped around the forest clearing.

"I think so," answered a little monster.

Katie watched from behind a

tree as the most amazing monsters appeared. They looked just like the ones she had seen in the story. They were very noisy, stomping about and making the funniest sounds. All the monsters turned to face Mongo.

"Hello, everybody. Welcome to our Monster Competition. I hope

you are all ready for some monster fun! Let's start with our first game. Take your places, everyone, for the Monster Muscle Game."

With that they all cheered and formed a long line behind a huge rock. Katie could not help laughing at them because they were so funny. They wobbled about making strange noises. One of them kept jumping high into the air.

"Boing!" called Mongo. "I know you're excited, but could you stand still for one minute?"

The monsters laughed as Boing turned a deep red.

Katie could not believe her eyes when the first monster lifted the huge rock high above its head and threw it into the air. Within seconds it landed by the tree, narrowly missing Katie's head.

"Help!" she cried.

"What was that? Who's there?" asked Mongo.

"It's me," replied Katie creeping out from where she was hiding.

"Look at that!" bellowed Boing.

"What a funny looking creature," laughed Fang.

"It's all arms and legs," giggled Roly.

"What is it?" asked Boggle.

"What do you mean?" replied Katie. "I'm a little girl, my name is Katie and I don't look half as funny as you!"

"Pleased to meet you," said
Mongo. "Where did you come
from?"

"Well, I was lying in bed
looking at my monster poster,
thinking about all the adventures
you have when suddenly I found
myself in the picture. I was just
watching your game when that
rock very nearly squashed me,"
explained Katie.

"I'm glad you like our stories
and I'm sorry you nearly got hit,
but nobody knew you were there.
Why don't you come and join in
our games?" suggested Mongo.
"I'm sure you'll make an

excellent monster."

"But I couldn't lift that rock, let alone throw it," laughed Katie.

"Well, we can find you one just the right size," said Mongo.

One by one, the monsters threw the rock as hard as they could to see who could throw it the furthest. Last was Katie with a much smaller rock, which she threw with all her might. The monsters cheered. Boing said, "Well done. You're a great monster. You'll love the next game."

All the monsters, including Katie, had to stand in the stickiest mud, and make a set of footprints. Then they each had to guess which set belonged to which monster. It was great fun, but they all got in a terrible mess, which Katie particularly enjoyed.

Next came the roaring game, each monster roaring as loud as it could. "Aaarrrggghhh!" went the first one. "Gggrrraaawww!" went the second. Then it was Katie's turn. "Yaa!" she shouted.

"Louder," giggled Mongo. "You can growl louder than that. Roar right from your toes."

"Ymaaa!" roared Katie, and everyone clapped.

"Well done," shouted Fang.

"Am I making a good monster?" asked Katie.

"One of the best," laughed Fang. "You're a natural."

"What's next?" Katie asked Mongo.

"It's my favourite one. It always makes me laugh till I cry," he said, chuckling. "It's the funny face competition. Each monster stands in front of the others and pulls silly faces."

"No problem. I'm good at pulling faces. I practice all the time at home," she giggled.

"Good. Then again you've got a funny face anyway. You've only got two eyes, one nose and a mouth. That's funny enough," said Mongo, and they both laughed.

They watched as the monsters pulled the most hilarious faces. They all laughed and laughed. But when it was Katie's turn they were all rolling on the ground and holding onto their tummies. They had never seen anything so funny.

After the last game the prizes were given out. Katie won first

prize for the funny face game. Mongo pinned a gold star onto her pyjama jacket. Then they all danced and sang and had a great party.

Suddenly, Katie heard a loud ringing noise and turned to see where it was coming from. It was her alarm clock.

She was lying in bed, all twisted up in her duvet.

"Oh! I don't want to be back here. I was enjoying my monster adventure," she said to herself. As she untangled herself from her duvet she let out a cry. "Ouch!" She had pricked her finger on something sharp. She looked down at her pyjama jacket and saw the small gold star. "Oh wow! Then it wasn't just a dream!" Katie jumped out of bed and went over to her poster.

All the monsters were there as before, as well as a small girl behind a tree.

"It's me!" Katie gasped. She thought she saw Mongo wink.

"Thank you. I had a lovely time. It'll be our secret," she whispered. Just then Katie's mum came in to say good morning.

"Hello, Katie. Sleep well?" asked Mum.

"The best ever," replied Katie. Mum looked down and saw mud all over Katie's feet.

"Look at your feet! They're filthy! Go and wash them at once. Whatever have you been doing?" asked Mum.

"Just dreaming," replied Katie, as she winked at Mongo.

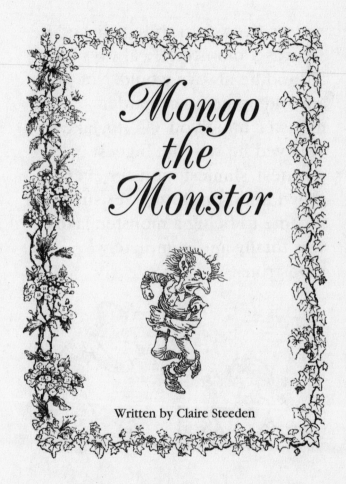

Mongo the Monster

Written by Claire Steeden

JAKE KEGWORTH truly believed he was a monster. He always had and he always would. Not just any old common or garden monster, mind you. Oh no, Jake believed he was the biggest, meanest, slimiest monster ever to growl, snarl or glower. Yes sir, when it came to being a monster, Jake was totally and completely monstrous.

Of course, there were certain monster-type things that he was unable to do. He wasn't allowed to eat his younger brother, Michael, for instance. He had thought about it once or twice (usually in the middle of the night, when eighteen-month-old Michael — with whom Jake shared a bedroom — was crying for attention or food, or whatever it was baby brothers cried for at such unsociable hours). But Jake's mother had made it quite clear to him that even the meanest of monsters did not eat their younger brothers, nor any member of the family for that matter.

Neither was Jake able to leave

slime trails in his wake. This was a particularly sore point with him, as Jake believed this to be the most basic of monster habits. But once again, Jake's mother was adamant!

"There are to be no slime trails left around our nicely decorated house!" she would say, before looking skywards with that peculiar kind of look that only exasperated mothers can give. And naturally, Jake's complete lack of slimy tentacles, along with his quite normal amount of eyes, arms, legs and so on, did put something of a damper on his efforts to scare the living daylights out of Mrs Ricklesworth, his elderly next door neighbour. Jake was, of course, a young monster, so his view of Mrs Ricklesworth's age was not quite accurate. In everybody else's eyes — including her own — she was in her late forties.) No matter how often he waved his arms about, or writhed and wriggled his fingers in what Jake felt was a distinctly creepy manner, Mrs Ricklesworth remained quite unnervingly cool.

"Ah!" Jake thought, in his darkest moments. "But if I had even

one purple tentacle, things would be very different. Oh yes! "

Despite all this, Jake still believe-ed himself to be much better at being a monster than anybody else he knew — although he would occasionally and grudgingly admit to himself that Mr Pink, the mathematics teacher at Jake's school was not too far behind him in the monster stakes, even if he did have a silly name for a monster!

Now although Jake believed himself to be a monster, few other people took him at his word. Can you believe that? Despite all the evidence Jake had at his disposal, when he referred to himself as a monster his friends would just laugh and say:

"If you're really a monster, Jake, where are all your monster friends?"

So it was that one morning, Jake decided to put all doubts of his monster-hood to rest.

He went to the *Yellow Pages* and scoured the listings, he looked for Monster Taxis and Monster Dry Cleaners and even Monsters For Hire, but he couldn't find a hint of anything even vaguely connected to monsters!

His friends, watching from outside the window, were most

curious to know why Jake was looking so intently through the phone book.

"Perhaps he's going mad?" one of them suggested.

They were even more bewildered when Jake let out a yelp of delight and began jumping around the room in a most peculiar manner. They watched as he dashed to the telephone and made a call. When Jake had finished, one of his friends tapped on the window. Jake rushed over, threw the window open and declared,

"You are all invited to tea on Saturday, when I shall prove to you once and for all that I'm a monster!"

Naturally enough, word spread around the town that something was going to be happening on Saturday and everyone became excited at the thought of Jake making a very large fool of himself.

"Perhaps this will finally free the poor boy from the crazy idea that he is a monster! It would make my life a lot more peaceful, I can tell you!" Mrs Ricklesworth said to her good friend, Mrs Parker (about whom we shall perhaps talk some other time, when you will learn of the fate that befell her husband during an attempt to cross the English Channel on a raft made of sponge-cake).

Saturday came (as Saturdays do) and brought with it a 1arge crowd of interested onlookers gathering around the Kegworth household. The crowd became more and more excited as the afternoon wore on, calling for proof of Jake's monster status. In fact, they became so loud that Jake's poor mother developed the most frightful headache!

Jake's friends arrived for tea at five minutes before four o'clock, each of them looking a little nervous, if truth be told (and of course, it is). And at four o'clock precisely, everyone, including Mrs Ricklesworth, Jake's family and friends and all of the interested onlookers, fell into a hushed silence. What was about to happen? What was Jake about to do?

By five minutes after four, the crowd was getting restless, and murmurs of "I told you so," could be heard. Nothing had happened, of course!

How silly of them to think that something would. Poor Jake was beginning to look a little green (which is something that all good monsters know how to do, by the way).

Just then, a large, brightly paint-ed coach drew up outside the house.

And what do you think happened? Well, I'll tell you ... the coach doors opened and out walked the most revolting bunch of monsters you've never wanted to see (or perhaps you have, in which case you may well be a monster, too!)

They were slimy, nasty, icky and yucky looking, with all kinds of tentacles, claws, eyes on stalks, lumps and bumps. It's fairly safe to say, that they were an unbelievably ugly bunch, even by monster standards, and they are pretty low!

They made their way up the garden path and Jake opened the front door

"Hello, my friends!" he said.
"How nice to meet you all at last!
Do come in and have some tea!"

"Hello, Jake!" said the biggest
monster, through at least sixteen
mouths. "I hope you've got some
chocolate biscuits, because as you
probably know, monsters simply
adore chocolate biscuits!"

Sure enough, Jake had
chocolate biscuits, along with all
kinds of other nice things to eat.

They all sat down to tea, and
neither Jake's family, his friends or
the rest of the town, ever doubted
again that Jake was a true monster!
After all, who else but a monster
would invite other monsters to tea?

Now you might be wondering how Jake eventually contacted the other monsters? It was really very simple, he looked in the phone book under "Clubs and Associations" and found the number for the "Monster Society and Social Club". If you'd like, you can give them a call and invite some monsters round for tea, but you'd probably best check with your mother first, because as Jake's mother found, monsters really do leave slime trails everywhere they go!

Granny Casts a Spell

SUSIE WAS very fond of her Granny. Each day, when Susie got home from school, Granny was always there sitting by the fire knitting. Granny knitted so fast that sometimes it seemed as though the knitting needles sparked in the firelight.

"Do you know," Granny would say, "that I'm really a witch?" Susie always laughed when Granny said that because she didn't look at all like a witch. She had a smiling face and kind eyes and she never wore black. Not ever. When Granny wasn't looking, Susie would take a peek inside her wardrobe just in case she might find a broomstick or a witch's hat. But she never found so much as a book of spells.

"I don't believe you're a witch," said Susie.

"I am," replied Granny, "and I'll cast a spell one day. You'll know when that day comes, for my needles will start to knit by themselves." After that, Susie kept a careful watch over Granny's needles, but they always lay quite still in the basket of knitting.

One day, Susie was playing in her garden when she heard the sound of weeping. The sound seemed to be coming from under the old tree in the corner. She walked towards the tree and as she did so the crying noise got louder,

but she could not see anyone there.
Then she looked down at her feet
and there — sitting on a mossy
stone — was a tiny little man. He
was neatly dressed in a yellow velvet
waistcoat and knickerbockers. On
his feet were beautiful, shiny,
buckled shoes, and a three-cornered
hat with a wren's feather in it
trembled on his shaking head. When
the little man saw Susie, he stopped
crying and started to dab his eyes
with a fine lace handkerchief.

"Whatever can the matter be?"
asked Susie, crouching down.

"Oh dear, oh dear!" sobbed the
little man, "I am the fairy princess's
tailor and she has asked me to make

her a lovely gown to wear to the
May Ball tonight, but a wicked elf
has played a trick on me and turned
all my fine gossamer fabric into bats'
wings. Now I shall never be able to
make the princess's gown and she
will be very angry with me." He
started to cry again.

"Don't cry!" said Susie. "I'm
sure I can help. My Granny's got a

sewing basket full of odds and ends. I'll see if she's got anything nice for a party dress. I'm sure she won't mind sparing some — after all, you won't need much," she said. At that, the little man looked a bit more cheerful.

"Wait here," said Susie, "while I run indoors and see." She ran up the garden path and in through the back door.

"Granny, Granny!" she called. She ran into the sitting room expecting to find Granny knitting by the fire. But Granny had her eyes closed and she was whispering to herself. On her lap was her knitting — and the needles were moving all by themselves, so that the yarn danced up and down on the old lady's knees.

For a moment, Susie was too astounded to move. Then she thought, "I hope Granny's not casting a bad spell. I'd better make sure the little tailor is alright."

She ran back down the garden path and there under the tree sat the tailor, surrounded by a great pile of gorgeous gossamer, shining in the sunlight.

"I've never seen such fine material — ever!" he exclaimed. "But where did it come from? I just closed my eyes to dab them with my hanky and when I opened them again — there it was!"

"I don't know," said Susie, "but I think my Granny might have had something to do with it."

"Well, I'd never be able to thank her enough," said the tailor. "For now I shall be able to make the finest gown in the whole of fairyland. The princess will dance the night away in the prettiest dress there ever was." He paused and then went on, "I'm

also indebted to you, for it was you who helped me in the first place. I would like it very much if you came to the May Ball, too."

"Why, thank you so much," Susie replied, "I should like that very much." She didn't want to hurt the tailor's feelings but she knew she couldn't go — she was far too big to go to a fairy ball!

"Well I must get on with the dress now," said the little man, reaching for a pair of fairy scissors. "See you tonight!" And with that he vanished.

Susie went indoors again. Granny was knitting by the fire as usual. Susie wondered if she had dreamed the whole thing. Everything seemed so normal. Really, how could she have imagined she'd seen a fairy tailor in the garden! And as for Granny casting a spell!

That night, Susie lay in bed and wondered if the fairies really were having a ball. How she longed to be there! Once she thought she heard a tapping at the window. Was that the fairy tailor she saw through the glass — or was she imagining it? In the middle of the night she awoke with a start. There was a click, clicking noise at the end of her bed.

"Granny is that you?" called Susie.

"Yes, dear," replied Granny.

"I couldn't sleep, so I decided to do some knitting. All at once the needles started twitching, so I knew it was time to cast a spell. What is your wish, Susie?"

"I... I...," stammered Susie, "I want to go to the May Ball," she blurted.

"Then you shall, my dear," said Granny.

In an instant, Susie felt herself

shrinking and when she looked down she saw she was wearing a beautiful gown and tiny satin slippers. Then she floated on gossamer wings out through the window and off to the Ball.

The next morning, Susie woke up in her bed. Had it all been a dream — the revelry, the fairy food, the frog band, the dance with the fairy prince? Then she saw something peeping out from under her pillow. And what do you think it was? It was a tiny, tiny shred of the finest gossamer fabric.

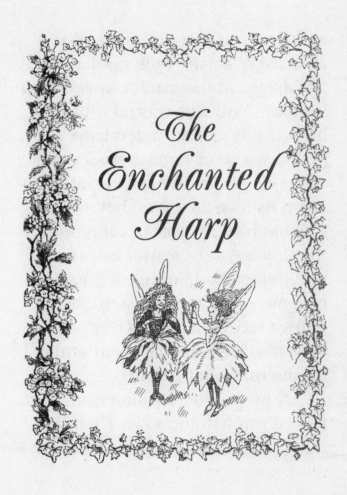

The
Enchanted
Harp

LONG AGO there lived a pedlar.
Every day he took up the same
place in the market square with
his harp. Now this was no ordinary
harp. It was an enchanted harp. The
pedlar would call out to passers-by
and, for a penny, the harp would play
all on its own any tune they wished.
It could play any sort of tune from
the slowest, most tearful ballad to
the liveliest, happiest jig. It could
play music for any occasion. Sometimes a wedding party would come
by just to have the harp play a tune
for the bride and groom.

Now one day a young man
passed through the town. He heard
the sound of the harp's sweet music

coming from the market square and made his way over to where the pedlar stood. He couldn't believe his eyes or his ears! The harp was playing a lullaby for a lady with a baby that was crying. The music was so enchanting that the baby soon stopped wailing and was fast asleep. Then he saw an old man give the pedlar a penny and whisper in his ear. The harp changed its tune and now it played an ancient melody that the old man had not heard for many a year, and his eyes filled with tears of gratitude.

The young man watched all this and thought to himself, "If only that harp were mine. I cou make a lot more money with it than that silly old pedlar!" He waited a while for the crowd to disperse, and then when he thought no-one was looking he went up to the pedlar and said, "People say that on this day a great spotted pig will fall out of the sky and land on the market square. Keep a look out and if you see a pair of trotters in the sky, get out of the way fast!" And he pointed up at the sky. The pedlar peered upwards but all he could see were scudding white clouds.

While he was staring up, the young man snatched the harp and was out of the market square and away down the street before the pedlar realised what had happened.

"Stop! Thief!" the pedlar shouted. But it was too late. By the time folk gave chase the young man had gone. He didn't stop running until he reached a town many miles away, where no-one had seen the enchanted harp before.

The young man set up the harp and called out to passers-by, "Two pennies and my harp will play any tune you wish!" A man and woman came up and asked for a waltz and, sure enough, the harp began to play. The couple spun round the square merrily and were happy enough to give the young man two pennies.

More and more people came by and asked for tunes. The young man rubbed his hands with pleasure. "I shall surely make my fortune now," he said to himself.

Weeks passed and the young man did, indeed, make a lot of money. He didn't care at all how much he charged. If someone who looked wealthy came along he might charge them six pennies or even eight. By now he had completely forgotten that he had stolen the harp and that it didn't belong to him at all. He bought himself fine clothes and ate expensive food and generally considered himself rather clever.

Then one day an old man in a

broad-brimmed hat came past and asked for a tune. He grumbled a bit when the young man asked for two pennies but held out the coins, making sure the young man could not see his face — for he was the pedlar!

"I'd like the harp to play a tune to drive you mad," said the old man.

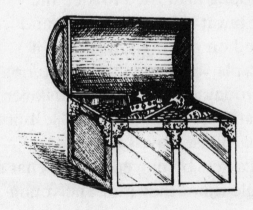

The young man thought this was a strange request but he had taken the coins and the harp had already started to play. It played a short and very silly tune. Then it played it again. And again. And again. And again. It simply wouldn't stop. By now the old man had slipped away, so when people weren't watching the young man tried to kick the harp, but it side-stepped him and carried on playing. On and on it went, playing that infuriating tune. The young man put his hands over his ears to block out the noise, but the harp just played louder.

Passers-by moved away. "What a terrible tune," they said. The young man tried to move away, too, but the harp just followed him down the road, still playing.

Everywhere he went, night and day, the harp followed the young man until he was at his wits' end. He had used up all his money and he was in despair. Finally, he thought there was only one thing to do. He must go back to the pedlar and beg him to stop the harp.

It took him a while to make his way back to the town where the pedlar lived, but sure enough there he was, standing in the market square trying to sell a few old pots and pans to passers-by. He looked very unhappy, and the young

man felt truly sorry for what he had done.

He approached the pedlar with the harp still playing away behind him. He was about to explain when, to his surprise, the pedlar stopped him and said, "I know all about your plight. I will stop the harp playing its maddening tune on one condition."

"I'll do anything," said the young man.

"You must ask people what tune they would liked played and then you must give them a penny each time."

The young man gratefully agreed and the pedlar told the harp to stop playing. The young man had to work very hard to earn enough money to give people their pennies, but he was willing to do so in return for the pedlar making the harp stop playing that maddening tune!

The Lonely Mermaid

THERE ONCE lived a mermaid named Miriam who was very lonely. All day long she sat on a rock combing her long, yellow hair and singing to herself. Sometimes she would flick her beautiful turquoise fish tail in the water and watch the ripples spreading far out to sea. Miriam had not always been lonely. In fact, she used to have a pair of playmates called Octopus and Dolphin. Octopus had gone off to another part of the ocean to work for the Sea King. He was always much in demand because he could do eight jobs at once — one with each arm. Dolphin, meanwhile, had gone away to teach singing in a school of dolphins. Miriam once thought she heard his lovely song far away across the ocean and she hoped in vain that he might come back and play.

One day Miriam was sitting on her favourite rock as usual. "How lonely I am," she sighed to her

reflection as she combed her hair and gazed at herself in the mirror.

To her astonishment, her reflection seemed to answer back. "Don't be lonely," said a voice. "Come and play with me."

Miriam couldn't understand it at all. She peered into the mirror and then she saw, beyond her own reflection, another mermaid! She was so startled that she dropped the mirror and her comb and spun around.

Miriam was puzzled by the sight in front of her. For there, sitting on the next rock was another mermaid — and yet she didn't look like a mermaid in many ways. She had

short, dark, curly hair and wore a
strange costume that definitely
wasn't made of seaweed. When
Miriam looked down to where the
mermaid's fish tail should have been,
she wanted to burst out laughing.

For instead of a beautiful tail, the

other mermaid had two strange limbs like an extra long pair of arms stretching down.

The other 'mermaid', who was really a little girl called Georgie, was equally amazed by the sight of Miriam. She had seen pictures of mermaids in books before, but now she couldn't quite believe her eyes. For here, on the rock beside her, was a real live mermaid!

For a moment they were both too astonished to speak. Then they both said at once, "Who are you?"

"I'm Miriam," said Miriam.

"I'm Georgie," said Georgie.

"Let's go for a swim," said Miriam. Soon the two of them were in the water, chasing each other and giggling.

"Let's play tag along the beach," suggested Georgie, and started swimming towards the shore. She had quite forgotten that Miriam would not be able to run around on dry land. Miriam followed though she was rather afraid, as her mother had always told her not to go near the shore in case she got stranded. Georgie ran out of the water and up on to the beach.

"Wait for me!" called Miriam, struggling in the water as her tail thrashed about. Then, to her astonishment, something strange happened. She found she could leave the water with ease and, looking down, saw that her tail had disappeared and that in its place were two of those strange long arm things like Georgie's.

"What's happened?" she wailed.

Georgie looked round. "You've grown legs!" she shouted in amazement. "Now you can play tag!"

Miriam found that she rather liked having legs. She tried jumping in the air, and Georgie taught her to hop and skip. "You can come and stay at my house, but first I must find you some clothes," said Georgie, looking at Miriam who was wearing nothing but her long, yellow hair. "Wait for me here!"

Georgie ran off and soon she was back with a tee shirt and shorts. Miriam put them on. They ran back to Georgie's house together. "This is my friend Miriam," said Georgie to her mother. "Can she stay for tea?"

"Why, of course," said Georgie's mother.

"What's that strange thing?" whispered Miriam.

"It's a chair," said Georgie. She showed Miriam how to sit on the chair. All through teatime Miriam watched Georgie to see how she should eat from a plate and drink from a cup and saucer. She'd never tasted food like this before. How she wished she could have

chocolate cake at home under
the sea!

After tea Miriam said, "Now I'll
show you how to do something."
Taking Georgie by the hand she led
her down to the beach again. There
they picked up shells, and then
Miriam showed Georgie how to
make a lovely necklace from shells
threaded with seaweed. While they
made their necklaces, Miriam
taught Georgie how to sing songs of
the sea.

Soon it was bedtime. "You can
sleep in the spare bed in my room,"
said Georgie. Miriam slipped in
between the sheets. How strange it
felt! She was used to feeling water

all around her and here she was
lying in a bed. She tossed and
turned, feeling hotter and hotter, and
couldn't sleep at all. In the middle of
the night she got up and threw open
the window to get some fresh air.
She could smell the salty sea air and
she began to feel rather homesick.
Then she heard a familiar sound
from far away. It was Dolphin calling
to her! The noise was getting closer
and closer until at last Miriam knew
what she must do. She slipped out of
the house and ran down to the
beach in the moonlight. As soon as
her toes touched the water, her legs
turned back into a fish tail and she
swam out to sea to join Dolphin.

The next morning, when Georgie woke up, she was very upset to find that her friend had gone. When she told her mother who Miriam really was, her mother said, "The sea is a mermaid's true home and that's where she belongs. But I'm sure you two will always be friends."

And indeed, from time to time, Georgie was sure that she could see Miriam waving to her from the sea.

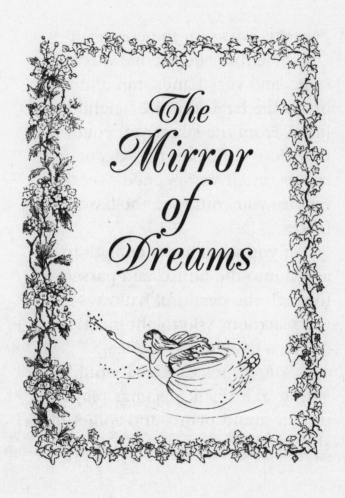

The Mirror of Dreams

THE HOUSE on the corner of Nightingale Avenue was tall and very handsome, and was by far the largest in the neighbourhood. From the street you could see four floors of beautifully decorated rooms, and if you peeped over the railings you could see the basement below.

If you were lucky enough to be asked into the house, and passed through the beautiful hallways into the playroom, you might meet the owner's daughter, Cordelia.

Sometimes Cordelia would be sitting in her silk pyjamas playing on her grand piano, and sometimes she would be dressed in the finest velvet gowns playing with her lovely dolls.

If you went down the stairs and into the basement, you might come across Polly. Polly's mother was a chambermaid in the house, and worked hard all day long to make the house sparkling clean. Sometimes Polly helped her to polish the ornaments and dust the furniture, but more often Polly sat on her own in her small bedroom drawing pictures with some crayons on a drawing pad she had been given for her birthday. When Polly was helping to polish the furniture she would look longingly at all of Cordelia's fine clothes and toys, and when she sat

alone in her room she would draw
pictures of all the beautiful things
she would like to own if only she
could afford them.

One day, a large parcel was delivered to the house and taken upstairs to Cordelia's bedroom. A little while later, Cordelia's maid carried a pretty, ornate mirror down from her room and put it with the rubbish waiting for collection outside the house. Polly asked the maid why the mirror was to be thrown away, and the maid explained that Cordelia had been given a new mirror in which to brush her long, silky locks, and that she didn't need it any more. The maid then asked if Polly would like the old mirror, and of course Polly accepted with pleasure — it was the most beautiful thing she had ever owned.

Polly carried the mirror back to her room and polished it lovingly. As she polished the glass a strange thing started to happen. The glass went misty, and then cleared as her own reflection stared back at her once more. But the reflection that stared back was not dressed in rags and worn old clothes as Polly was, but in a rich gown of the most beautiful cream satin, with pink bows and apricot lace.

Polly was entranced. She looked almost as beautiful as Cordelia! Her hair gleamed and her fingers were white and magnificent. As she looked further into the mirror, she saw herself dancing at a ball, and then sitting down to eat the finest food she had ever seen — hams and roasted meats, and cakes of strawberries and cream!

And then the mirror spoke to her. "I am the Mirror of Dreams," the cool, clear voice said. "Whatever your heart desires most will be reflected in my shiny surface."

Polly was astounded, but so happy. She didn't care that it was only a day dream, for when she saw her reflection in the beautiful clothes, she felt as if she were truly there dancing and eating the fine foods — she could almost taste the fruit and cream in her mouth!

From that day on, Polly sat in

her room every day, and dreamed
and dreamed and dreamed. She had
never felt so happy before, and could
not wait to wake up each morning
to visit her imaginary world. She
certainly didn't understand how
Cordelia could have thrown away
such a magical wonder, and thought
that she could not have known of its
enchanting secret. She supposed also
that Cordelia could have had no use
for such a mirror, for whatever
Cordelia wanted in real life she
received, and would have no need to
dream. But Polly was to find out that
this was very far from true!

Weeks passed, and every day
Polly sat and dreamed of ermine

cloaks, of diamonds and pearls, of parties and picnics and carnivals. Eventually, she had dreamed every dream she had ever wanted. And Polly began to realise that it no longer made her as happy as it once had, and she began to grow weary of her Mirror of Dreams. She sat in front of the mirror less and less, and eventually when she did visit the mirror she could not think of a single thing that would make her happy. Even the dreams she had in which her mother wore fine silk clothes and didn't have to scrub and clean for their living could no longer make her happy.

She preferred her real mother,

who came to kiss her good night and read her stories no matter how tired and overworked she was. Eventually she stopped looking in the mirror altogether, and finally decided to throw the mirror away — it had only made her more unhappy.

As the long winter turned into spring she acted upon her decision, and took down the mirror to throw away with the rubbish. But as she looked into the glass, it misted over in its familiar way and she saw herself in the mirror as she looked in real life, but in it she was playing with other children like herself, and reading stories with them and sharing toys. She felt gloriously happy, and knew in that instant that all she wanted was a very good friend. She realised in that moment, too, that perhaps Cordelia really had known the mirror's secret, but that she also had become more unhappy as the dreams faded and reality forced itself upon her. She wondered aloud what it was that Cordelia had dreamed of, and for the second and last time the mirror spoke in its cool, clear voice.

"The Mirror of Dreams showed Cordelia her heart's desire, and her heart desires a true friend and companion — someone who is not jealous of her wealth, but a friend who will share her hopes and dreams, and with whom she can have parties, games and picnics."

Polly put the mirror down and thought with amazement that she could be that friend, if Cordelia would be friends with someone poor but honest and true. Polly left the mirror with the household rubbish and was about to make the descent back to the basement, when she saw Cordelia standing in the garden at the back of the house. Cordelia had seen her discard the mirror, and shyly walked up to Polly. Polly overcame her shyness also and went to meet Cordelia, and then she told her they shared the same dream.

Cordelia and Polly became the best of friends from that day on. They shared everything they had, no matter how much or little. They talked and laughed together all day long, and they played long into the evening. They didn't have to dream any more, for they had both got their true heart's desire.

The Giant Who Shrank

ONCE UPON A TIME in a far-off land, there lived a huge giant. He made his home in a big cave high up in the mountains. His bed, table and chairs were made from great tree trunks. And when he wanted a drink, he simply filled an old bath tub with water and drank it down in one enormous gulp. When he snored — which he did almost every night — it sounded like a huge thunderstorm, and the noise echoed all around the mountains.

At the bottom of the mountains there was a village, but all the folk in the village were very different from the giant, for they were not big at all. They were just like you and me.

They were afraid of the giant, of course, and whenever he came striding down the mountains to hunt, they all ran away into the woods or locked themselves inside their houses. Sometimes, the clumsy giant would tramp around the village squashing houses with his great feet as he went, and that only made the village folk even more frightened of him!

Although the giant was so big and strong, he was not a bad giant, but he was very, very lonely because everyone ran away whenever he appeared. Sometimes, while he was sitting alone in his cave, he could hear the villagers having feasts and parties and he longed to join them and be just like them.

One day, when the giant was tramping around the village as usual, something glinting in the sun caught his eye. At the top of a big tree (which of course was not very big as far as the giant was concerned) lay a gold box.

The giant bent down and picked up the box. To his surprise he heard

a small voice inside say, "Help! Help!
Let me out!"

The giant opened the box and
out jumped an elf. "Thank you, thank
you, large sir," he said. "I am a magic
elf, but one of my spells went wrong
and I got locked inside this box.
No-one in the village could hear
me calling for help high up in
this tree."

To show his thanks, the elf said
he would grant the giant one wish.

"I wish I could be the same as
all the other villagers," boomed the
giant.

"What a difficult wish," said the
elf. "You are so big! But I will do my
best."

The elf closed his eyes and chanted a magic spell. But nothing seemed to happen — the giant was still as big as ever.

The giant was very sad to discover that he had not shrunk, but he wished the elf well, thanked him for trying and went on his way. As the giant was walking back to his cave in the mountains, he noticed something strange. All the puddles of water that he had passed on the way

down to the village had got bigger.
They were as big as lakes now!
The giant looked up to see if it had
been raining, but the sky was clear
and blue.

Then another strange thing
happened. The big stone steps he
had cut in the mountain side leading

up to his cave had also got bigger!
He could hardly clamber up them.

Eventually, puffing and panting,
the giant reached the door to his
cave. But he could not reach the
door knob. It now towered above
him, far from his reach.

"What is happening?" thought
the giant. "The elf's spell must have
gone wrong. Not only am I still a
giant, but everything around me has
now got even bigger."

Suddenly the truth came to him.
Of course! Everything had not
become bigger — he had become
smaller! The spell had worked after
all. Now he was just the same as the
other folk in the village.

He made his way to the village, wondering if everyone would still run away as before. But he need not have worried. All the village folk welcomed him into the village, and he lived there happily among them for the rest of his days.

The Naughty Broom

GOODNESS ME, what a lot of dirt and dust there is all over this kitchen floor," said the maid. She was a very house-proud maid, and didn't like dirt and dust on her floor one little bit. Out came the broom from its place in the cupboard in the corner, and soon the maid was busily sweeping the floor and brushing all the dirt and dust into a big dustpan.

Unfortunately, this kitchen also had elves living in it. They were too tiny to see, of course, but if you upset them they could be very mischievous indeed. As the broom worked away, it swept into one dark corner where the elves were having a party. Suddenly the king elf was swept away from their little table and into the dustpan! The next thing he knew he was being thrown, with all the other rubbish, on to the rubbish tip.

Coughing and spluttering with rage, the king elf finally climbed out from under all the rubbish in the rubbish tip and stood on top of it. He picked the dirt and dust out of his ears and nose, pulled a fish bone from out of his trousers and tried to look as king-like as he could, having just been thrown on to a rubbish tip. "Who did this?" he squeaked at the top of his voice. "I'll make someone very, very sorry indeed," he vowed.

Eventually he made his way back to the house, and into the kitchen again. The other elves looked at the king elf and did their best not to laugh. For the king elf was still looking very dirty and untidy, and still had bits of rubbish stuck all over him. But the other elves knew better than to laugh at the king, because he was likely to cast a bad spell on them if they did.

"It was the broom that did it," chorused all the other elves.

"Right," said the king elf, "then I'm going to cast a bad spell on the broom."

The broom was by now back in its cupboard. The king elf marched over to the cupboard and jumped in through the keyhole. The king elf pointed to the broom and said,

"Bubble, bubble, gubble, gubble,
Go and cause a lot of trouble!"

And with that the broom suddenly stood to attention, its bristles quivering. It was night time now and everyone in the house was asleep. The broom opened its cupboard door and sprang into the kitchen. It then unlocked the kitchen door and went outside. Straight to the rubbish tip it went, and with a flick of its bristles, swept a huge pile of rubbish back into the kitchen. Tin cans, dirt, dust, chicken bones and goodness knows what else all got swept on to the kitchen floor. The broom then closed the kitchen door, took itself back to its cupboard and all was quiet until morning.

When the maid came down into the kitchen, she couldn't believe her eyes. "Who has made this awful mess?" she said. "If I find out it was those cats . . ." she threatened. She took the broom from the cupboard and swept all the rubbish back outside again.

The next night, the same thing happened. Once it was quiet and everyone in the house was asleep, out of its cupboard came the broom, and into the house came all the rubbish again, swept there as before

by the naughty broom. This time,
there were fish heads, old bottles
and all the soot from the fireplaces.

Well, the maid was speechless.
After clearing up again, she got the
gardener to burn all the rubbish
from the rubbish tip, so that nothing
else could be brought in — although
she still had no idea how it had
happened.

That very night, the naughty broom decided it would make a mess in a different way. So instead of sweeping in rubbish from outside, the broom flew up to the shelves and knocked all the jars to the ground. With a crash they fell to the floor, one after another, and spread their contents everywhere.

"Stop this AT ONCE!" demanded a voice suddenly.

The broom stopped its mischief.

"What do you think you are doing?" said the voice again. The voice had come from a very stern-looking fairy who was now standing on the draining board, with her hands on her hips. What the broom did not know was that one of the bottles it had knocked down contained a good fairy, imprisoned by the elves. Now she was at last free, the spell was broken and it was her turn to cast a spell.

"Broom, broom, sweep this floor,
Make it cleaner than ever before.
Find the elves that cast your spell,
And sweep them off into the well,"
she chanted.

The broom went to work. It seemed to sweep so fast that its bristles just became a blur. Into this corner it went, then into that, and into every nook and cranny it swept. Every bit of dirt and dust, and all the broken bottles, were swept into the

dustpan and then out of the house.
Then it came back and swept all the
elves down into the well where they
couldn't do any more mischief.

In the morning, the maid came
down to find a spotlessly clean
kitchen. She was puzzled to find
some of the jars missing, but
between you and me she was also
rather pleased. It just meant that
there were fewer things to dust.